Martine Oborne

One Gorgeous Baby

illustrated by Ingrid Godon

MACMILLAN CHILDREN'S BOOKS

Take one
lovely smile,

two
beautiful eyes,

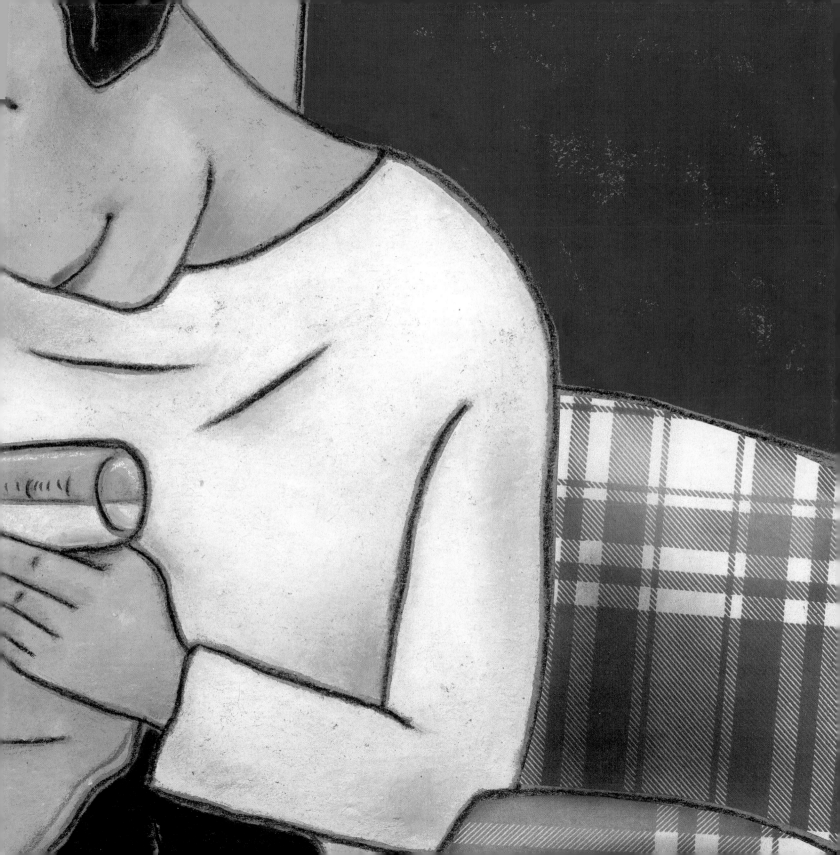

three big bananas,

four clean
nappies,

five cuddly toys,

six shiny buttons,

seven

bumpy

steps,

eight noisy ducks,

nine juicy
strawberries

and ten
sticky fingers!

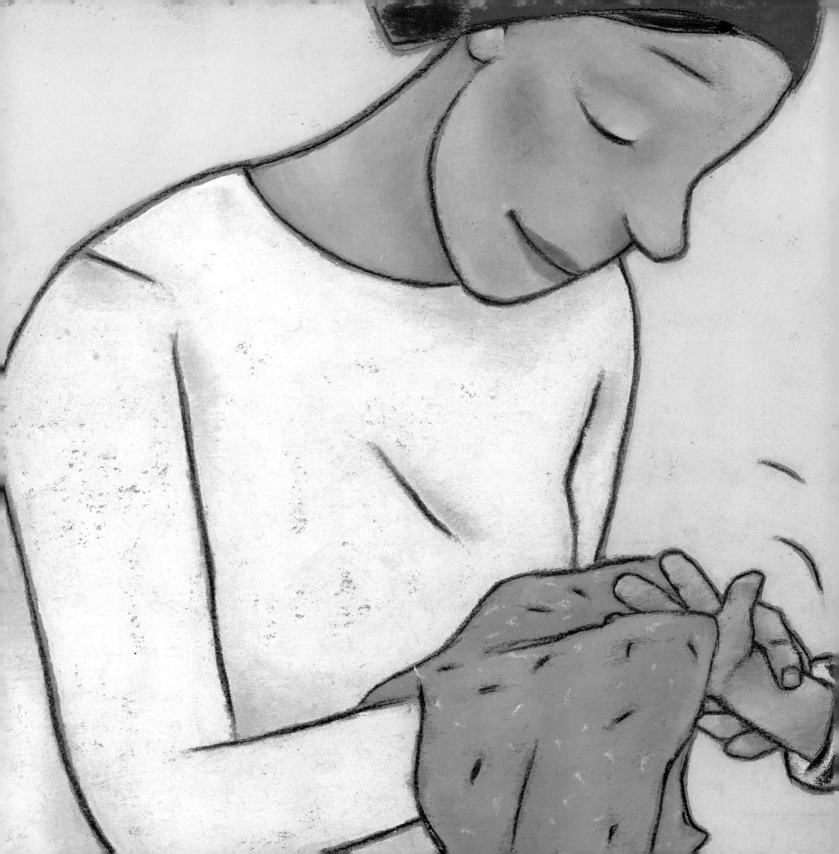

Put them all together and what do you get?

One gorgeous
baby!

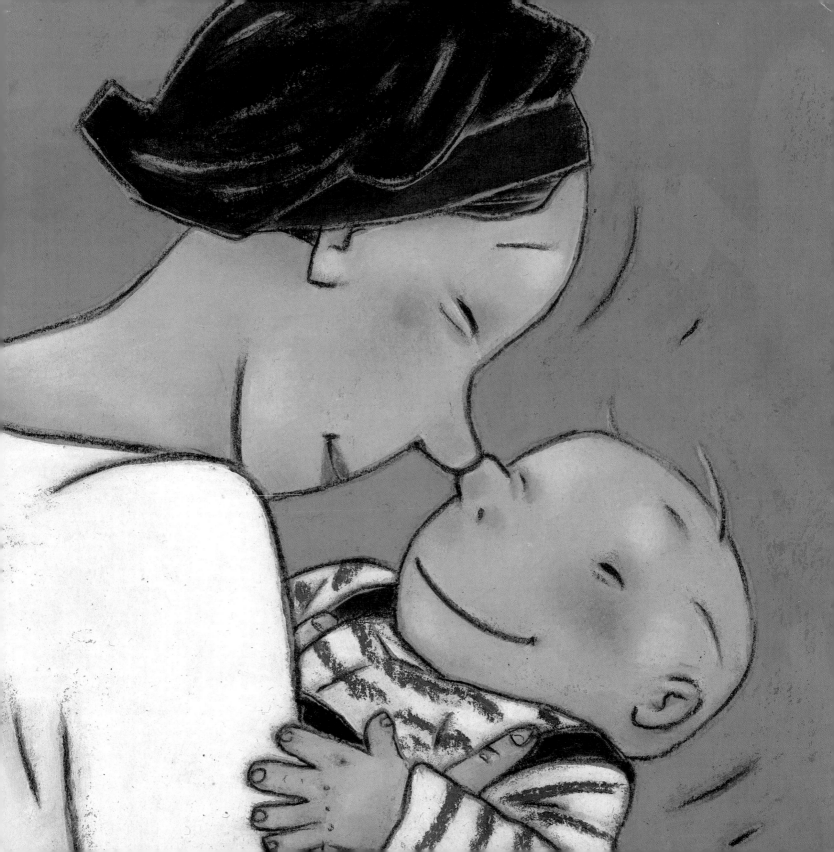

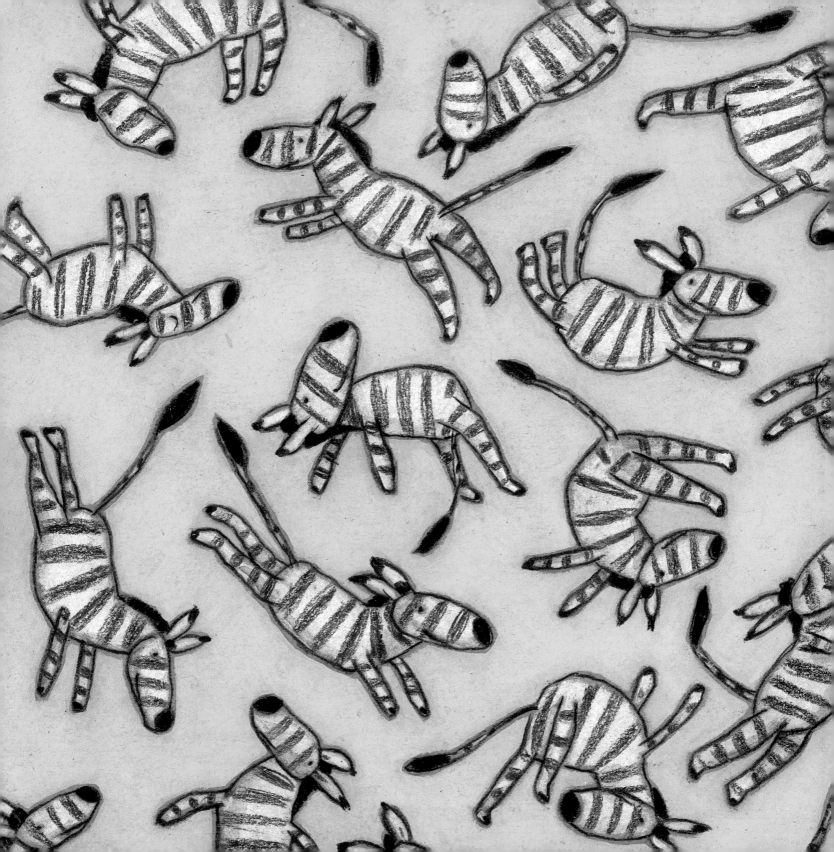